NO. AR.

MVFOL

The Strange Museum:
Men in Green

Strange Family Home

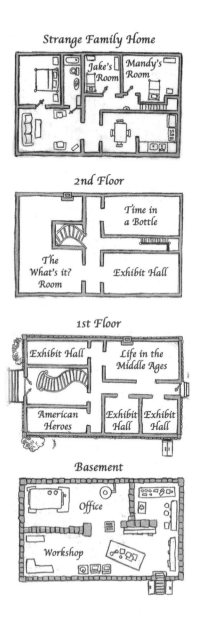

Jake's Room

Mandy's Room

2nd Floor

The What's it? Room

Time in a Bottle

Exhibit Hall

1st Floor

Exhibit Hall

Life in the Middle Ages

American Heroes

Exhibit Hall

Exhibit Hall

Basement

Office

Workshop

STRANGE MUSEUM

The Strange Museum

Men in Green

Written by
Jahnna N. Malcolm

Illustrated by
Sally Wern Comport

Gateway Learning Corporation
2900 S. Harbor Blvd., Suite 202
Santa Ana, CA 92704

ISBN 1-931020-10-8

First Edition
10 9 8 7 6 5 4 3 2

Nobility isn't a birthright, it's defined by one's actions.

—Robin Hood, Prince of Thieves

Contents

Chapter One
The Rope Climb

Jake pulled on the rope. Then he took a deep breath. This was it. If he didn't reach the top here, he'd never be able to do it in his P.E. class.

All week long the kids at Yorkton Middle School had been taking fitness tests in P.E. It was all anyone talked about at lunch, between classes, or after school. Kids compared running times in the 50- and 100-meter dash. They took turns showing each other the techniques they used in the broad jump. They even bragged about how

1

they could do more sit-ups than the required fifty.

But there was one event no one liked to talk about. That was the rope climb. It was the final test, and the one almost everyone bombed. Many kids had rope burns on their hands. One boy had reached the top but fell seconds later. His body hit the padded mat, but his head hit the wood floor. He had to get three stitches.

Jake's sister Mandy was in 8th grade and had taken the rope test two years before. But she was no help to him.

"It was the most embarrassing moment of my 6th grade year," she told him. "I was a total weakling. The coach made me try over and over again. But I couldn't even get started."

Jake had run really slow times in the 50- and 100-meter dash. He fell on the broad jump, and he had faded badly on the 400 meters. His friends were starting to tease him by calling him the "Turtle" and "His Slow-ness." No way was he going to screw up the rope climb.

When Jake told his dad about his fear, Dr. Strange was ready to help. "Hey, I know just what you're going through, son," his dad said. "I had to take a test like that when I was in school. It took me two years to live it down."

It was his father's idea to turn one of the rooms at the Strange Museum into a gym.

"We are in the middle of putting up a new display in there, but there's lots of room," he said to Jake. "I'll hang a rope from the ceiling so you can practice. We can even get a mat, so if you fall, you won't hurt yourself."

It was lucky for Jake that his father was a scientist and an inventor. Many of the objects that came into their museum were in bad shape, but Dr. Strange was always able to fix them. He always found ways to hang unusual objects in their museum, so he knew how to rig the rope to the ceiling. Dr. Strange set it up on Thursday morning.

When Jake got home from school that afternoon, the rope was ready. Normally, Jake and Mandy worked at the museum on Thursday afternoons, but his mom said he could take the day off to practice.

Mandy thought that was a stupid idea. "Oh,

please! Like you're going to turn into an Olympic champion overnight? I think you're just doing this to make me have to deal with the Pink Ladies all by myself."

Groups like the Pink Ladies often arranged for tours at the Strange Museum of Lost and Found. Usually Mandy and Jake loved giving those tours. But the Pink Ladies were a group of old, cranky women who always wore something pink, like a hat or scarf or sweater.

"They are just a bunch of old grumps," Mandy said to her mom. She sounded like a grumpy old lady herself. "They always say they can't hear me when I talk. Last time I had to shout my way through the whole tour. I almost lost my voice."

Jake chuckled. "I spend most of my time taking them to the bathroom. Or the water fountain. I don't think they're interested in the museum at all. Maybe they just want to get out of the retirement home."

Mrs. Strange listened to her kids complain and smiled. "Those ladies may sound grumpy, but you should read the letters I get from them. They love the museum. And they love you kids. They always ask about you."

Jake looked at Mandy and made a face. "Just our luck."

"What are you complaining about?" Mandy said. "You get to swing from a rope all afternoon."

"Hey! You think that's fun?" Jake replied. "I'm in training."

Mrs. Strange handed Mandy a packet of information. "Be sure and tell the Pink Ladies about our newest display. It's called Life in the Middle Ages," she said. "It'll be set up in the room where Jake is, um, training."

"Oh, really?" Mandy turned to look at her brother. "Are any of the displays there now?"

"Yes," Mrs. Strange said. "We've hung several tapestries on the walls."

"What's a tapestry?" Jake asked as he tied his tennis shoes.

"You know, those big carpets with pictures on them," Mrs. Strange replied. "Oh, right. I knew that," Jake said.

"You should take a look at them," Mrs. Strange added. "They're exquisite."

Mandy gave Jake a sly smile. "Maybe we will."

"We?" Jake repeated. "What do you mean, *we?*"

Mandy wiggled her eyebrows. "That's for me to know and you to find out." She ran out of the room before Jake could get her to explain.

An hour later, Jake was on the second floor of the museum, staring up the long corded rope. The ceiling looked a million miles away. He had tried and tried but still couldn't pull himself more than halfway up the rope. "I'm going to give this one more try," he muttered as he wiped the sweat from his forehead. Jake wrapped his hands around the rope and took a deep breath. "Okay. Here goes nothing."

Jake inched his way a few feet up the rope— and froze.

There was a commotion just outside the door. He heard voices and footsteps, and one other sound—the little *thunk* of canes on a wood floor. It was the Pink Ladies! Mandy had brought them upstairs to watch Jake die of embarrassment.

Jake held his breath, hoping the group would keep moving past the door.

No such luck.

Mandy led the Pink Ladies into the room and declared, in a really loud voice, "And now, presenting my brother—Sir Falls-a-Lot."

Chapter Two
The Pink Ladies

Jake lost his grip and slid all the way to the mat. He hit the floor with a loud *thump*.

The Pink Ladies clapped their hands. "Wonderful! Simply wonderful."

Jake was speechless. The sudden drop had knocked the wind out of him. Mandy didn't say a word either. She was bent over at the waist, snorting with laughter.

When the clapping died down, Jake found enough air to gasp, "All right, ladies. Show's over. It's time to go."

Mrs. Griffin, who was the oldest lady in the group, held up her hand. "Isn't this the Life in The Middle Ages room? I thought we were going to see crossbows and armor, and things of that nature."

Mandy wiped the tears off her cheeks. "Yes, Mrs. Griffin," she said. "This will be the Life in the Middle Ages room. But the display is not ready yet. My parents are still setting it up."

"But isn't this young man part of the show?" another lady asked. "He should be. The Middle Ages were a time when men lived in the forest and swung from vines."

"That's right, Mildred," another lady chimed in. "And they hunted their food with bows and arrows. And they played music on those odd stringed instruments."

"You must mean a lute. That's one right there." Mandy pointed to a stringed instrument with a round back that had been hung on the wall. "It was made in England over 1000 years ago. I think this one was played by the lords and ladies of the court."

"Love songs," Mildred said, clasping her hands to her chest. "That's what they used to play for each other!"

Jake and Mandy gave each other a look that said, "I think Mildred's really lost her marbles."

A bell sounded and Mrs. Strange's voice came over the loudspeaker. "Ladies and gentlemen, the Strange Museum will close in five minutes. Please exit through the doors in the front lobby. Thank you for coming."

"Five minutes!" Jake repeated. "You guys better run. At five o'clock the museum doors are locked and, if you're still in here, anything could happen."

Mandy crossed her eyes at her brother, then herded the Pink Ladies out the door and down to the front lobby. She waved good-bye on the front steps, then raced back to the Life in the Middle Ages room.

Jake was still standing by the rope, looking angry.

"Got you!" she called with a grin.

"Maybe for now," Jake shot back. "But you're going to be sorry you ever came in here."

Mandy faked a yawn. "Oh, like I'm really scared."

"You would be if you lived in the Middle Ages," Jake said. "Why, if a guy's sister played a dirty trick like that on him, he'd do something she'd never forget."

Mandy put her hands on her hips. "Like what?"

"Like . . . like . . . hit her with a—" Jake

looked around him for something big and scary
from the display. He spotted a longbow hanging
on the wall. The bow was almost six feet long and
made of a very thin strip of wood. It was too
flimsy.

But the lute on the other wall looked like an old-
fashioned guitar with a round back. If he hit his
sister with that, it would hurt a lot more than the
bow. Jake grinned and reached up to take the lute
off the wall.

Mandy's eyes widened. "Jake, don't touch
anything!"

"Oh, you're scared, are you?" Jake said.

Mandy nodded. "You bet I'm scared. Jake,
it's after 5 o'clock."

"So?"

"So the museum is closed," Mandy reminded
him. "You know what Mom and Dad have told us."

"Don't touch a thing," Jake said in unison
with Mandy.

"And you know what can happen if you do,"
Mandy warned.

Jake rolled his eyes. "Of course."

When he had touched the map in the American Heroes room, the two of them had suddenly been transported two-hundred years back in time. They'd met Paul Revere and helped warn the Americans that the British soldiers were coming.

A month later Mandy was the one who forgot the rules and touched an old tin lantern in her father's workshop. That mistake had sent them to the stormy coast of North Carolina where they met Blackbeard the pirate.

Jake stood with his fingers just inches away from the lute. He looked at the clock on the wall. It was ten after five. If he touched the lute, something strange would probably happen. He looked at Mandy's face. All the color had drained out of it. She was definitely afraid.

"Don't do it," Mandy whispered. "We may never come back."

Jake wiggled his fingers. He liked having the power to scare his sister. "I won't touch this lute on one condition."

"What?"

"That you give all the tours to the Pink Ladies for a whole year."

"What? That's not fair!"

Jake moved his fingers closer to the lute. "Want me to touch it?"

"No! I'll do it." Mandy put her hand over her heart. "Cross my heart and hope to die, I'll take the Pink Ladies for the entire year."

A smile spread slowly across Jake's face. "All right then."

He lowered his hand and turned to go. Unfortunately his foot got tangled in the rope hanging from the ceiling.

"Jake!" Mandy cried. "Look out!"

Jake jerked back and forth, trying to get his foot loose. Then he fell back against the wall with a crash. Above his head the lute slipped off its hook and started to fall to the floor. Without thinking, Mandy dove forward with her arms out. She and Jake caught the lute at the same time.

Before Jake could cry, "Oh, no, we did it *again*!" the room began to spin. A sound like a runaway train roared in their ears.

Jake and Mandy shut their eyes and felt themselves pulled out of the Strange Museum, and back through time.

Chapter Three
The Man in Green

When Jake and Mandy opened their eyes, they were standing in the middle of a great forest. Giant oaks soared above them, their huge trunks covered with dark green moss. Mandy was still in her museum T-shirt and short skirt. Jake was still in his T-shirt and gym shorts. Both of them still held the lute.

"If you value your life," a voice behind them warned, "you won't move."

Jake and Mandy ignored the warning and turned to look.

Facing them was a handsome man dressed in green. He wore a shirt and leather vest over a pair of green leggings. A short dagger hung from the belt. Perched on the top of his head was a pointed green cap with a long feather in it.

His bow and arrow was aimed straight at Jake's heart.

"Something tells me this isn't Peter Pan," Jake muttered out of the corner of his mouth.

"What was your first clue?" Mandy shot back. "The bow and arrow? Or the knife?"

"Careful, he might hear you," Jake hissed.

"I don't care if he hears me!" Mandy spat out her words angrily. "I told you not to touch that lute. And what did you do? Touch it. Now we're about to be target practice for some nut in tights."

"I beg your pardon!" The man shifted the aim of his bow. Now the arrow was pointed at Mandy. "What did you call me?"

Mandy gulped and answered in a low voice, "Um, I guess I called you a nut in tights."

"That is what I thought you said," the man replied. "Now that we've established who *I* am, please do me the favor of telling me who *you* are."

The man sounded light-hearted, but the point of the arrow stayed aimed at them the whole time he spoke.

"Let me talk," Jake told his sister. "You're making a total mess of things."

Mandy folded her arms across her chest. "Fine. Tell him who we are and how we got here. I'm sure he'll believe *you*."

Jake took a deep breath. "I am Jake Strange and this is my sister, Mandy Strange. We're the Strange children."

A sound like a chuckle came from the man in green. "That much seems clear," he said.

"Strange is our last name," Jake explained. "And believe me, it's no fun having that name. Everyone makes fun of us."

Mandy jabbed him with her elbow. "He doesn't want to hear that."

"Anyway," Jake continued, "one second I was practicing for a test in my house, and the next minute, I was here."

"Are you saying you are lost?" the man asked.

"Yes," Mandy cut in. "We are so lost that we don't know where we are, or *when* we are."

The man looked confused. "What do you mean?"

"What my sister is trying to say is that she is not sure what year this is." Jake laughed nervously. "In fact, we were just having a little disagreement about it. Maybe you could clear things up for us."

For the first time, the man lowered his bow. Just a little. "The year, my young friend, is 1191."

"What!" Mandy gasped. "That's impossible. Why, that's over 800 years ago!"

Jake quickly put his hand over his sister's mouth. "Don't mind my sister. She is a big joker."

Jake tried to sound calm, but his insides felt like a popcorn popper. They had traveled back in time over 8 centuries. That was just too far from home!

Mandy's knees felt weak. The same wild thoughts that Jake was having rushed through her head. If they *had* gone back 800 years, then where were they? They couldn't be in America. At that time, only Indians lived in America.

She pulled her brother's hand off of her mouth. "Excuse me, sir, but what country is this?"

The man blinked in surprise. "You don't know the year, and you don't know the country. Did you both receive a blow to your heads? This country is England. And you are standing in Sherwood Forest."

"Sherwood Forest," Jake repeated. "I know that place."

"Good for you!" the man said. "Maybe your wits are returning."

Mandy had heard of Sherwood Forest, but she couldn't quite remember where.

"I've seen it in a lot of movies," Jake turned to his sister. "And so have you."

Mandy bit her lip trying to think. It was hard to think with an arrow pointed at her heart.

"Oh, come on, Mandy," Jake said. "Look at the man in green. You know who he is."

"Well, he looks a little like the Jolly Green Giant," Mandy said, "except he's not a giant."

Jake rolled his eyes. "Think!"

The man lowered his bow and smiled at Jake. "Oh, you've heard of me, have you?"

"Almost everyone knows you," Jake said to the man in green. Then he put his face close to Mandy's and whispered, "I'll give you a hint. His first name is Robin."

"Right you are!" the man replied. "I am Robin of Lockslee."

"Robin of Lockslee?" Jake repeated. "That's not who I mean."

"It's not?" The man looked a little disappointed.

"No." Jake shook his head. "The guy I'm talking about lived in Sherwood Forest and was called Robin Hood!"

The man raised one eyebrow. "Really?"

Jake nodded. "He took money from the rich and gave it to the poor."

"Did he?" The man in green leaned against a tree and crossed his arms. He looked very interested.

"He didn't do it all by himself," Jake went on to explain. "He had a group of guys that helped him. They were called his Merry Men."

"Were they?"

Jake waved one hand. "But of course you aren't him. That guy didn't really exist. He was just a legend, something a writer made up in a book."

"They write books about this man?" the man in green asked.

Jake nodded. "Lots of books. But it's really pretty stupid. I mean, who would believe that a bunch of guys in green lived in trees in the forest."

"Jake," Mandy warned, but Jake rambled on.

"And nobody really takes from the rich and gives to the poor—"

"Jake!"

"Merry Men in jolly old England," Jake continued. "That's a laugh."

"JAKE!" Mandy shouted so loud that her brother jumped.

"What?" Jake demanded.

Mandy pointed up. Jake slowly raised his head to look.

Filling the treetops were nearly twenty men. All of them were dressed in green. And each one

had a bow and arrow aimed right at Jake
and Mandy.

Chapter Four
The Not-so-Merry Men

hen it's true!" Jake cried. "You really are Robin Hood!"

The man in green bowed at the waist. "I must confess, that *is* my name. But I do not like strangers using it."

"And strangers are not welcome in Sherwood Forest," a gruff voice said. The voice came from a big man standing on a branch above the children.

"I think my friend Will Scarlett is telling you to leave these woods," Robin Hood said. "If I were you, I'd listen to him."

Mandy was totally ready to get out of Sherwood Forest, and England, too. And she knew just how to do it. "Here!" She held out the musical instrument. "Take back your lute and we'll be on our way."

Robin cocked his head to look at the instrument. "That's not my lute."

"Oh, don't be silly! I'm sure you must have lost it," Mandy said, pushing it toward him. "Please take it back."

"Don't touch it, Robin," a short, round man called from his perch in a nearby tree. "It's a trick."

Mandy stared at the lute, and then at her brother. He looked as confused as she felt. Always before, when they had traveled back in time, it was to return a lost item to its owner. Paul Revere had lost part of his map, and when they gave it back to him, they came home. A lantern had sent them to the shores of North Carolina, where they met a girl named Tess. When they returned her lost lantern, they were transported home. Why wasn't the same thing happening this time?

Jake frowned. "Are you sure you don't play

the lute?" he asked Robin.

"Sad to say, I have not the talent nor the desire to play a lute," Robin said with a shrug. "Sorry."

"*Now* what do we do?" Mandy asked.

Jake took back the lute. "We have to find the person who lost this lute and give it back to them. That's the only way we're going to ever get home."

"Then be off with you now!" the man named Will Scarlet yelled from above them. "Or I'll see to it that you never leave these woods." He shook his bow at them angrily.

Robin cupped his hands around his mouth and shouted up to the big man in the tree. "Calm down, Will. Can't you see these are only children?"

"If they are just children," the man shot back, "then why are they dressed in such strange costumes? I think they must be players from a circus. Or worse, strangers from another country."

"Try another century," Jake muttered under his breath.

"They're spies!" another man cried, raising a large stick. "Sent to sniff us out and betray us."

This caused a howl of loud protests from the

other men as they shouted the word, "Spy! Spy!"

Robin held up one hand and the forest fell silent. "Use your brains, lads. These children are lost and upset. And I think I know why." He walked slowly around Jake. "You see, they have clearly been the victims of thieves. This poor boy was robbed of his clothes. He was sent into the woods in his undergarments."

Jake looked down at his bright blue gym shorts and bare legs. He suddenly felt like he was standing in his underwear. He tried to hide behind Mandy.

Then Robin Hood pointed to Mandy. "And those same villains cut off this young girl's skirt and tied her hair behind her head."

Mandy felt her face turn red. She put her hand to her hair and tried to tug on the hem of her short skirt. "That might have happened," she said. "I don't really remember."

Robin clapped his hands together and looked at his men. "There! You see? They have each suffered a blow to the head, which has robbed them of their memory."

Jake nodded eagerly. He hoped the Merry

Men would believe Robin. He wasn't too keen on getting an arrow through the heart.

Will shook his head. "I still think these two children should leave the forest, Robin. The more people who know about our hideout, the more likely we are to be caught."

Robin Hood stood for a moment, rubbing his chin. "My friend Will makes a very good point," he said finally. "It is not safe for you to be here. All of us could get hurt as a result."

Mandy did *not* want to stay in these woods. They were dark and creepy. The sky was completely blotted out by the thick canopy of leaves above their heads. She felt certain that wild animals lurked behind every tree. But she was not keen on the idea of being sent off alone. "Um, excuse me, Mr. Hood," she said, raising one finger. "But where should my brother and I go?"

"Back where you came from!" another man in green called from the woods. "And you can take your germs with you, too!"

Robin smiled kindly at them. "Don't mind him. He has no fondness for strangers either. He says they bring danger and disease. And more often than not, he's right."

Robin motioned to the short, round man hiding behind a thick growth of bushes. "Tuck! Take these two to the highway. Direct them away from Prince John's castle."

The man stood up and nodded. "As you wish, Robin."

Jake and Mandy looked at each other confused. This was it? They had just met Robin Hood. Now they were being sent away? It didn't make sense.

"We'll do as you say, Mr. Hood," Jake said, trying to stall for time. "But I really think we should stay with you."

"That's not possible," Robin answered. He took Jake's hand and shook it firmly. "Tuck will find you some clothes to put on, and then you can be on your way. Good luck to you both!"

Robin bowed to Mandy. Without thinking, she curtsied back. Before they knew it, the two time travelers were walking through the woods behind the short round man called Tuck. He wore a long brown robe and worn leather sandals. A piece of knotted rope served as his belt.

Tuck had collected two long capes from the other men. He handed them to Jake and Mandy. "Put these on," he said. "They'll make you look decent. When we come to the highway, I'll leave you. Speak to no one about what you have seen here today."

"Right," Mandy said as she tied her green cape around her shoulders. She watched her brother struggle with his dark brown cape. It was a little too long and touched the ground.

Once Jake had gotten his cape tied, he said, "I know the story of Robin Hood and his Merry Men. But I don't remember why you guys are hiding in the forest. Can you fill me in?"

Tuck blinked at him in surprise. "We hide from the evil Prince John. He has given orders to get rid of all men who support his brother."

"And who is his brother?" Mandy asked.

Tuck put one hand on Mandy's forehead. "That must have been a mighty blow to your head for you not to remember," he said. "John's

brother is Richard, the true king of England. But he is away and has not been heard from for some time. We hear he is ill."

Jake snapped his fingers. "I get it! Prince John wants to be the king."

"Exactly."

"And you and Robin Hood don't want him to be king."

A dark cloud covered Tuck's face. "No one wants John to be king. He is a terrible, cruel man. He steals money and land from his people and gives back nothing."

By now they had come to the edge of the forest.

"Just beyond the line of trees lies a road," Tuck said. "Follow it to the west. You'll be safe then. I must leave you now."

Mandy turned to say good-bye, but the round little man was gone. They walked out onto the road. It was really just two narrow ruts that had been made by heavy carts.

"This is some highway," Jake commented as he and Mandy stepped onto the road. It was choked with rocks and puddles. "I wonder if they have a problem with speeding?"

The joke made Mandy smile, but only for a minute. Across a vast meadow in the distance she could see a gray stone fortress. Somehow she knew the grim tower was the castle of Prince John. But that's not what made her smile disappear.

It was the sight of forty mounted soldiers galloping straight at them.

"Run, Jake!" Mandy screamed. "Run!!!"

Chapter Five
Bad Prince John

Jake heard his sister's warning, but he could not get his legs to move. He felt like he was back on the rope in gym class—frozen in place. Jake stood in the middle of the road, clutching the lute to his chest and staring at the approaching horsemen.

As the horses thundered closer, they could see the man leading the charge. He had a short pointed beard and long dark hair that poked out from beneath his soft cloth hat. His clothes were purple, and much finer than those worn by the

soldiers riding behind him. His long velvet coat hung past his knees. His black leather gloves matched his tall boots.

The man raised one gloved hand and all twenty soldiers pulled their horses to a stop.

"You there!" the man barked at Jake and Mandy. "How dare you cross the Prince of England's road! I didn't give you my permission."

"The Prince of England?" Mandy gasped. "Prince John?"

The man nodded.

Mandy quickly pulled Jake into the ditch and bowed. "Sorry, sir. We didn't know."

"That is a lie." The prince turned in his saddle to address his men. "These two peasants have lied to my face."

"We mean no harm," Mandy said. "We're just poor travelers."

"Another lie," he said with a sneer. "If you are traveling, where is your bag? Where are your things? All you carry is a lute."

Mandy's eyes brightened. Maybe Prince John was the one who had lost the lute. If she gave it to him, they could go home. "Here, sir," she said, offering the prince the lute. "Is this yours? We're looking for its owner."

Prince John turned back to his men. "Do you see how clever they are? Trying to bribe me with a lute. Well, it won't work. Arrest them, and get them out of my sight."

Two of the soldiers hopped off their horses and ran towards Jake and Mandy. Their heavy swords clanked against their legs as they ran.

Jake had seen enough old movies to know what would happen to them next. First he and Mandy would be thrown into some dark prison cell with no food or water. They might even be chained to the wall by their ankles. Then years would go by. No one would help them. They'd grow old and crazy. Jake would probably grow a long gray beard and lose all his teeth. No way was he going to let that happen!

"Stand back!" Jake grabbed the lute and swung it by the neck like a baseball bat. "Don't come near us!" he shouted as he swung wildly.

The soldiers drew their swords. The sharp

blades glinted in the sunlight.

"Jake!" Mandy hissed. "Stop doing that or they'll stab you. And me!"

"That's better than growing long beards and losing our teeth!" Jake cried, still swinging.

"What are you talking about?" Mandy demanded as she tried to duck out of the way of the lute.

"Prison!" Jake shrieked. "They're going to put us in prison."

"Not today they won't," a voice called from behind them.

From out of nowhere Robin Hood darted forward and jumped onto the back of Prince John's horse. He pulled his knife and held it to the prince's throat.

"Tell your men to leave these children alone, John," Robin ordered. "And *perhaps* I will spare your life."

"Do as he says!" Prince John said quickly. "Now!"

The soldiers backed away but kept their swords drawn.

"That's better," Robin said, lowering his knife a little.

The prince's lips curled into a smile. "I thought I might see you today, Robin."

"Today? Why today?" Robin asked.

"Robin doesn't know the news," Prince John said to his soldiers. "What a surprise!"

The soldiers laughed as if they were in on a secret joke.

"You see, my dear Robin," Prince John continued, "today is the day that I will be crowned king."

Robin Hood looked like he'd been hit in the stomach. "But that's not possible," Robin said. "Richard is our king."

"My brother Richard is far, far away," Prince John said. "Word has it he's very ill. May die, in fact." He shook his head. "I'm quite sad about it, really."

"You can't get away with this," Robin said. "The people won't stand for it."

"The *people*?" When Prince John said the word, he looked like he'd eaten something sour.

"The *people* are all for it. That's why we're here. To greet the lords and ladies who have come for my coronation."

"That will never happen!" Robin cried, jumping backwards off the prince's horse. He slapped it on the rump and the horse reared. Then it bolted over the ditch and into the field, taking a startled prince with it. The soldiers wheeled about in confusion.

"Arrest him!" Prince John yelled as he tried to stop his horse. "Arrest them all."

Several soldiers leapt from their horses and ran toward the man in green.

"Run, children!" Robin cried as he took a sword away from the nearest soldier and held it in front of him. "Find my men!"

Jake and Mandy did as they were told. As they raced into Sherwood Forest, the children heard a battle rage behind them. All of a sudden there was a shout of victory.

"We're got him, Sire!" one of the soldiers cried with glee. "We've caught Robin Hood!"

Chapter Six
The Hideout

Help! Tuck!" Jake cried as they ran deeper and deeper into the forest. "They've got Robin Hood!"

Mandy ran as fast as she could, but she was barely able to keep up with Jake. Her brother was running faster than he'd ever run before. "If you ran this fast in the 100-meter dash," she huffed, "you would have gotten an A in P.E. class."

"Is anyone following us?" he asked, barking out his words between gasps for air. "Mandy, look behind you."

Mandy glanced over her shoulder. She didn't see anyone, but that that didn't mean much. The prince's men could be hiding. "I don't see them," she called, "or hear them. Where are we going?"

"As far into the forest as we can go," Jake said as they ducked under branches and hopped over thorny bushes.

Mandy was getting a pain in her side. She clutched it with one hand and called, "How are we going to find Robin's men?"

"We don't have to. They'll find us." Jake glanced up, hoping to see men in green ready to help them. Jake was so busy looking up that he didn't see the trap. There was a *snap!* and a *whoosh!* Before he knew what had happened, Jake was hanging upside down in the air by a rope.

Mandy stood totally still. As she looked around for another trap, she cried, "This is terrible!"

"No," Jake called as he swung back and forth above her head. "This is good. This means someone will find us for sure."

Mandy listened for the sound of Robin Hood's men moving through the forest. But

she heard nothing.

Jake's face was turning a bright red as the blood rushed to his face. "Check and see if those guards followed us."

Mandy tiptoed a few feet back the way they'd come. Then she held her breath and listened. At first she heard no sound at all. Then she heard something very odd. Music.

"What is that?" Mandy asked. "A radio?"

"A radio!" Jake tried to twist his body to look at her. "Nobody has a radio here. They haven't been invented. It'll be about 750 years before anyone even thinks of the idea."

Mandy cocked her head. She definitely heard music. She followed the sound farther into the woods. Finally she stopped in front of a large oak tree. "Jake! The music is coming from this tree!"

"I think you're losing your mind, Mandy," Jake said. "I don't hear any music. I only hear birds and bugs, and the blood rushing to my head."

Mandy walked in a big circle around the tree, turning her head this way and that. "I think it's a flute."

"Oh, really?" Jake muttered. "A flute inside a tree?"

Mandy nodded. "I know it sounds weird. But I hear a flute."

"Too bad I'm hanging upside down here," Jake said as he struggled to hold up the lute he was still carrying. "Otherwise I could join the flute player and we could form a band. A flute-and-lute band."

Mandy pressed her hand against the tree. It felt very warm. She got down on her knees and patted the bark. "Jake? This is a very strange tree." She pushed on a moss-covered spot and suddenly it swung open. With a cry, Mandy fell forward into total darkness.

"Mandy, wait!" she heard Jake wail from behind her. "Don't leave me here!"

Mandy found herself tumbling down a steep tunnel. She grabbed at tree roots to brake her fall, but they broke off in her hands. She rolled head over heels until at last she flopped to a stop.

She had kicked up a lot of dust with her

fall, which made it hard to see. When the dust cleared, Mandy saw that she was in a large cave. A cave filled with golden light. And she wasn't alone. Men, women, and even children sat together in little groups in the big rocky room. Some were at tables. Some stood at workbenches. They were all dressed in green and brown. They were Robin Hood's men.

"I know you!" a deep voice called from nearby. It was the man named Will. "What are you doing here? We just sent you out of our woods."

"Yes, sir, you did," she said as she pulled herself to her feet. "But Prince John's men stopped us on the road. Robin Hood came to help us, and now he's been taken prisoner. He sent my brother and me to find you and get help."

Will looked back at the tunnel. "Where's your brother, then?"

Mandy pointed behind her. "He's still up there. In a tree, hanging by his ankles. He's been caught in one of your traps."

"Hurry, lads!" Will gestured to two young men at a worktable. "Go and cut the poor boy down."

The two boys drew the blades from their belts and ran up the tunnel.

Mandy was about to go after them when Will caught hold of her arm. "It's not safe to follow. If Prince John has Robin, then his men are all over Sherwood Forest looking for the rest of us."

Mandy looked around at the faces lit by the light of lamps and candles. "How many of you are down here?"

"Well over a hundred," Will replied. "These limestone caves run a long way underground."

Mandy wanted to find out more about the women and children hiding in these secret caves, but her brother's voice stopped her.

"Mandy!" Jake cried as he stumbled down the tunnel into the cave. "You're alive. I thought you'd been eaten by that tree!"

Mandy laughed and threw her arms around his neck. "Are you okay? You had to hang upside down for a pretty long time."

Jake's face, which only moments before had been beet red, was now a pasty white. "I do feel a little woozy, but I think I'm okay. While I was hanging around up there, I discovered something pretty cool."

"What?"

"I'm not afraid of heights anymore."

Mandy cocked her head. "I didn't know you were afraid of heights."

"Why do you think I've never been able to do the rope climb?" Jake shot back. "I get halfway up the rope, look down and see how far I am from the ground, and freeze."

"Will!" a young boy called from the top of the tunnel. "Will!"

"What is it, Ned?" Will shouted back.

"I've come from the lookout," the boy said as he ran to join them. "There's a large party on the road riding for the castle."

"How many, boy, how many?" Will demanded.

"I don't know. Maybe fifty," Ned said. "But they're mostly lords and ladies, not men-at-arms."

Mandy nodded. "They're coming for the crowning of Prince John."

"What?" every man, woman, and child in the room gasped. "But that's not possible!"

"It's true," Jake added. "We heard Prince John tell Robin Hood about it. Just before he took him prisoner."

"When is this coronation to take place?" Will asked.

"Tonight," Mandy and Jake said together.

Will turned and faced his friends. The people in the cave stood in shock at the bad news. "Then we will all ride to the castle," Will said in a loud voice. "We'll rescue Robin and stop the coronation!"

Everyone in the cave, including Mandy, raised a fist in the air.

"To the castle!"

Chapter Seven
To the Castle

"Excuse me!" Jake shouted over the noise of the men gathering their bows and arrows. "EXCUSE ME!"

Everyone stopped what they were doing and looked at Jake.

"Before I go *anywhere* with a bunch of guys in green suits," Jake said, "I have to be certain of one thing." He held up the lute. "Does this belong to anyone here?"

"That's an odd question to ask," a young man with curly blond hair said.

Jake shook his head. "The answer will help me decide whether my sister and I should go to the castle, or just go home."

The young man cupped his hands around his mouth. "If this lute belongs to any of you, kindly raise your hand and come get it."

No hands went up. No one made a move toward Jake or the lute.

Jake shrugged. "Then I guess we'd better go to the castle."

Mandy peered at the tunnel that led to the forest. "Won't Prince John's men notice us when we all step out of that tree?" she asked the young man.

"We're not going that way," the young man said with a chuckle. "There is an underground passage that will take us all the way to a door inside the castle."

"That's fantastic," Jake said. "That way we can get in, get Robin, and get out, and no one will see us."

"A good plan, yes—except for one thing," Will said as he filled his quiver with arrows. "We don't have a key."

"The gate at the end of the passage is locked
from the castle side," the young man explained.
"One of us has to go through the main gate of the

castle, get the key, and unlock that door."

"So who's that going to be?" Jake asked.

Will clapped Jake and Mandy on their shoulders. "You two."

"Us?" Jake's voice cracked. "Why us?"

Will pointed to the lute. "Because you play an instrument, and because you are wearing strange clothes. With a few additions, you two could pass for travelling musicians, there to perform for the coronation."

Then Will turned to a tiny old woman in the group. "Nan, can you find them something festive to put on?"

"I'll do it, Will," she said.

Will turned to the young man with the curly hair. "And Curtis, Nan will give you a costume, too. You can play your flute."

"Flute?" Mandy repeated. She turned to Jake and whispered, "See, I did hear music."

"Wait a minute, wait a minute!" Jake protested. "You're not going to hear any music from me." He held up his lute. "I don't know how to play this thing."

"Ha! Ha! That's very funny, lad!" Will said, slapping him on the back. "Now be off with you."

Before Jake and Mandy could say another word, they were whisked into another room in the underground cave. Baskets full of wool and stacks of rolled cloth sat on the ground. Most of the cloth was brown and green, but one basket in the corner was full of clothes made of red and yellow satin and blue velvet.

Nan grinned at them, showing only one tooth on top and one on the bottom. "We took these from some very fancy lords and ladies," she said. "They were having a costume ball."

Mandy held up a few of the velvet dresses. They smelled bad. They had probably never been washed. She wondered if anything was living inside them. Like fleas or lice. Just the thought made her itch.

"Come on, you two," Curtis said as he put on a red and yellow jacket and grabbed a hat that looked like a big yellow turban. "We haven't a moment to lose."

Mandy shook out a blue velvet dress and

slipped it on over her clothes. Next she picked up
a square of white cloth that she draped over her
dark hair. Nan set a slim gold band on top of
Mandy's head to keep the cloth in place.

Jake was pickier. He couldn't decide between
the patchwork velvet jacket or the solid red jacket.
Mandy made up his mind for him. "Take the one
that looks like a quilt. People will be so busy
staring at your clothes, they won't have a chance
to notice you're not playing."

Ten minutes later, the three of them ran
down a tunnel to one of the cave's exits. When
they stepped into the light, Mandy could see that
they were very near the castle. The cave's door
was behind a large boulder and cleverly hidden
under the shrubs and leaves.

Curtis inched around the side of the boulder.
"We're in luck," he called. "There's another party
coming up the road now. A large group, too, with
several lords and ladies on horseback, and a troop
of servants following in a wagon and on foot. We'll
wait until they pass by and fall in behind them."

Mandy could feel her heart thump wildly in

her chest. What if the guards didn't let them in? What if they were thrown in prison? Or worse, killed on the spot?

Jake still had the lute. Mandy knew the only way they were going to get back home was to hand that lute back to its rightful owner. There wasn't any other thing to do but go into the castle.

"Hurry!" Curtis waved for them to follow. "Do what I do and step lively."

Mandy gulped when she saw the guards at the castle gate. There were four of them. They wore metal helmets and thick gloves. Their padded jackets and big leather boots made them look huge. Each carried a long spear with a nasty hook near the end. They all looked like they meant business.

"Try to stay calm," Curtis whispered out of the side of his mouth. "Look like you're here to celebrate."

Jake plastered a silly smile on his face and strummed the lute a few times as they neared the guard. Mandy tried to sing along with her brother, but the lute strings were badly out of

tune, and what he was playing didn't come anywhere close to sounding like a song.

Luckily Curtis was with them. He bowed low to the guards. Jake and Mandy quickly did the same. Then Curtis struck a pose and said, "If you open the gate, you shall feel no regret. This lady will sing, and this lad will fret!" He raised his flute to his lips and played a merry tune. The guards nodded their heads to each other and grinned. One of the guards waved them inside the castle gate. "Performers are to wait in the kitchens," he said.

"The kitchens?" Jake repeated as they hurried into the courtyard. "This is great. I'm starved."

But the moment they were ushered into the kitchens, he lost his appetite. Dozens of dead rabbits, ducks, and chickens hung by their feet from the roof beams. A large boar's head was on the table. They watched the cooks, who had stains all over their aprons, prepare dishes of food with filthy hands.

"Cancel what I just said," Jake said, trying not to gag. "I've decided to go on a diet."

Mandy shuddered and said, "I'm with you."

The dead animals and the dirty cooks didn't faze Curtis. He reached for a roll from a pile in a basket and said, "So, who holds the keys to this grand place?"

Jake turned to Mandy. "Does Curtis think he's being sneaky? Because he's not."

As Curtis took a bite of his roll, he whispered over his shoulder, "Trust me."

"I used to hold the keys," said an old man sitting on a stool in the corner. He was plucking feathers off a chicken. "But they took that duty from me when my eyes failed. Now it's Fat Tom who keeps the doors and locks for Prince John."

"Fat Tom?" Curtis repeated. "And where would he be?"

The old man shrugged. "Where else? In the Great Hall."

Curtis bowed and played a little tune on his flute. Then he gestured for Mandy and Jake to follow him. "Hurry. We need to find Fat Tom."

When they stepped into the Great Hall, Jake and Mandy both had the same reaction.

"Wow!" Mandy said.

Jake whistled. "Not just wow, but wow-*ee*!"

The Great Hall was twice the size of a basketball court. It could seat several hundred guests with no problem at all. Huge red banners hung down the stone walls. Each had a crouching lion woven in gold thread on it. The roof soared fifty feet above their heads. Thick wooden beams fanned out from the huge log that ran down the center of the roof.

Jake stared up at the roof and said, "I feel like I'm inside the belly of a giant whale."

The great dining hall was half filled with servants running around, getting the room ready for the coronation feast. It took only a few seconds to identify the man who held the castle keys.

Fat Tom sat on two benches in the corner. He held a drumstick in one hand and a huge pewter mug in the other. When he saw Mandy and the boys come towards him, Fat Tom stood up.

All three of them gasped at once.

"Fat Tom is a . . . is a . . . *giant*!"

Chapter Eight
Fat Tom

Mandy was certain she had never seen a man as big or as tall as Fat Tom.

He had to be over 8 feet tall. As for his weight, Mandy could not even take a guess. His hands and his feet were the size of pie plates. He had big, bulging eyes and a fiery red beard. She knew if someone was holding auditions for a play of *Jack and the Beanstalk*, Fat Tom would definitely get the part of the giant.

"We'll never get the keys from that guy," Jake said. "All he'd have to do is sit on us and we'd be toast."

Curtis didn't say a word. He watched the big man stride toward them. Then he put the flute to his mouth and played a tune that matched the rhythm of the man's steps. Several of the servants stopped and smiled. Jake flipped his lute over and played it like a drum. He looked at his sister and said, "If you know what's good for you, sing!"

The only song Mandy could think of that remotely matched the tune Curtis was playing was from her kindergarten years.

"The wheels on the bus go round and round," she sang.

"Round and round, round and round.
The wheels on the bus go round and round,
All around the town."

"Bus?" Jake raised an eyebrow. "Try a different verse."

Mandy took a deep breath and sang,
"The giant's steps go boom, boom, boom!
Boom, boom, boom! Boom, boom, boom!
The giant's steps go boom, boom, boom!
All around the, uh, castle!"

A silly smile came over Fat Tom's face. He began to bounce up and down with the song.

"He likes it!" Jake whispered. "Keep singing."

"No," Curtis cut in. "Dance."

"Dance? No way!" If there was one thing Mandy did not like to do, it was dance. Every time she tried to dance, she felt like a goon. She could feel her cheeks already starting to turn red.

"Dance!" Curtis ordered. "Don't you see the keys?"

Fat Tom stood between the long tables in the center of the Great Hall, clapping his hands and tapping his foot in time to the music. The ring of keys on his belt jingled and jangled as he bounced up and down.

"Go on, Mandy," Jake urged. "Dance *and* sing!"

Mandy was in a panic. The only dance steps she knew were from her sixth-grade square-dancing class, which she hated. But if she didn't do something quick, their chance to get the keys might pass. She took a deep breath and skipped to the middle of the dining hall. Then she folded her arms across her chest and danced around Fat

Tom in a "do-si-do."

"*The giant's keys go clang, clang, clang!*" she sang, pointing to his keys.

"*Clang, clang, clang! Clang, clang, clang!
The giant's keys go clang, clang, clang!
Let's hear them ring!*"

Fat Tom laughed as Mandy skipped around him. She pointed at his keys again and repeated her verse. This time he got the message. With a giggle, Fat Tom unhooked the key ring from his belt and shook it. Mandy took hold of the ring and they shook it together. She used the keys to pull him around in a circle, all the time singing, "*The giant's keys go clang, clang, clang! Listen to them ring!*"

Curtis saw that Mandy had her hand on the key ring and he moved closer, still playing his flute. Jake was right behind him, banging away on the lute.

Mandy knew this was the perfect time to run off with the keys. But where would she run? Fat Tom could catch her in two strides of his giant legs.

She and the giant kept spinning and spinning

in a circle. Her stomach felt funny and her head was getting dizzy. If she didn't stop soon, she was afraid she might throw up.

All at once Fat Tom let go of the keys. To Mandy's astonishment, she saw the huge man bow deeply at the waist. "Maid Marian," he boomed.

Mandy spun around to see who was there.

Standing in a shaft of light that came from an upper window was the most beautiful lady Mandy had ever seen. She was dressed in a deep green velvet dress with long sleeves and gold trim on the cuffs and neck. A gold chain was belted around her waist. A gold crown ringed her beautiful auburn hair. But it was her green eyes that caught everyone's attention. They looked like two glowing emeralds in the light. Mandy felt like she'd heard the lady's name before, but she couldn't remember when.

Everyone in the room was frozen in a bow when the lady said, "Please! Play on! Dance on! I love music!"

Curtis did what he was told and started a fast tune. Jake thumped away on the back of the lute and called, "Everybody dance!"

As the servants swarmed onto the floor of the
Great Hall, Mandy took that as her cue to leave.
She tucked the keys under her cloak and tried to
blend with the crowd. Curtis was stuck playing
the music. He hissed over his shoulder, "You must
get to the dungeon. The door is in the courtyard
next to the guardhouse. Release Robin, and he
will take you to the secret gate under the castle!"

Mandy was paralyzed with fear. "Jake!" she
begged. "You've got to come with me. I can't do
this by myself."

He nodded and called to the crowd, "Everyone
clap. That's right. Put your hands together—and
go for it!"

As the dancers, including the beautiful lady,
clapped their hands, Jake and Mandy slipped
out of the Great Hall into the courtyard. Off to
their right was the blacksmith's shop. To the left,
wooden racks covered with wet sheets and shirts
stood in front of the laundry. The guardhouse
was directly in front of them. They were in luck.
It was empty.

"Hey, wasn't that fun?" Jake said as they ran toward the entrance to the dungeon. "I mean, that was your basic Ye Old Rock Concert."

"This is not my kind of fun," Mandy said with shaky voice. "We have to find Robin and unlock the cellar gate before Fat Tom notices his keys are missing."

"My keys!" a voice boomed through the doors and windows of the Great Hall. "She stole my keys!"

"Too late!" Jake said as they raced down the dungeon steps. "We're toast!"

Chapter Nine
Unlock the Doors!

The dungeon was dark and damp and smelled of rotting things. Water dripped from the ceiling. Terrible moans and groans echoed down the passages. Mandy clung to Jake's arm as she followed him through the dark maze. She knew there must be rats lurking around every corner. She jumped every time she saw a shadow.

"How are we going to find Robin," Mandy whispered, "before Fat Tom and Prince John's guards find us?"

"There's only one way," Jake whispered back. He cupped his hands around his mouth and called, "Robin? Robin Hood! Are you here?"

Several voices shouted from all directions, "Yes! I'm here! Please, let me out!"

Jake and Mandy didn't know which one to follow. Then another voice called, "I'm Robin Hood. Who wants to know?"

They knew it was the real Robin Hood in an instant and ran to his cell. It had a small wooden door hinged into a stone wall. Robin was peering through a tiny window in the door.

"Are my men with you?" Robin asked as Jake tried one key after another in the lock.

"They're at an underground gate in the cellar," Mandy explained. "We're to get you out of here and unlock the gate."

Jake's hands shook as he fumbled with the lock. "I can't seem to find the right key," he cried as voices boomed from the stairs above. The guards were coming.

"Try the little one," Robin said. "Be quick about it, will you?"

The voices got closer. Mandy was about to choke with fear. "Hurry, Jake!"

Jake put the key in the lock, and the door opened.

Robin stepped into the hall, took the keys from Jake, and signaled for them to follow him. No one said a word as Robin led them through the maze of underground passages.

The guard's voices got louder and louder and Robin started running. So did Jake and Mandy. Finally Robin found what looked like a hole bashed into the wall near the floor. He squeezed through it and gestured for them to follow. Jake and Mandy crawled through and suddenly they were up to their ankles in moving water. It was an underground stream.

Robin straddled the stream and kept on running. "We're almost there," he whispered.

They turned a corner and found their way blocked by a heavy iron gate. The gate hung down over the stream. It had sharp points along the bottom, so the water could pass through but no one could climb under the gate into the castle.

"Where is everybody?" Mandy asked. "Will and the rest of your men were supposed to meet us here."

Robin Hood put his two fingers to his lips and whistled. In an instant the tunnel outside the gate was filled with people.

Robin rattled the keys at Will, who stood at the front of the crowd. Will grinned as Robin took the largest key on the ring and placed it into the lock. With a twist of the key, the lock clicked. Robin and Will heaved the gate upwards like a garage door. The rest of the Merry Men moved into the tunnel without a word. Some carried spears and short swords. Others had arrows ready to shoot. Mandy and Jake smashed themselves against the wall to let them pass.

Will handed Robin his bow and a quiver of arrows. Robin slipped them over his shoulder and said, "The guards are still in the dungeon. Take the men there." He looked at Jake and Mandy. "You two come with me."

"But where are we going?" Mandy asked, eyeing the open gate and the way out.

Robin was already running back the way they came. "This stream flows right under the kitchens and the Great Hall," he called over his shoulder. "We're going to stop the coronation."

As Jake moved to follow Robin, Mandy caught his arm. "Are you sure you want to go back into the castle? We're at the gate. We could get out right now."

"And miss out on a chance to help Robin Hood save the kingdom?" Jake said. "Not on your life!"

Mandy followed her brother and Robin back through the tunnel. As they passed the hole that led back into the dungeon, they could hear the clash of swords and angry shouts from the castle guards fighting Robin's men.

They ran on until they came to some big stone steps. Robin climbed them two at a time. Jake and Mandy scrambled after him. At the landing, Robin placed an arrow in his bow and said, "I'm going into the Great Hall. One of you must ring the bell in the tower. That will signal my men to join me."

Jake raised his hand. "I can pull on a rope.

That's easy."

Robin shook his head. "It is not that simple. You have to climb the rope to the top and ring the bell there."

Jake gulped. "Climb the rope?" Just saying the words made his knees go weak.

Mandy nudged him. "You can do it, Jake. I know it. And if you can't get to the top—" She took the lute from her brother. "I'll take this into the castle and see if I can find its rightful owner."

Robin took off his green felt hat and put it on Jake's head. "Take my hat. It's always brought me luck." Then he pointed through a stone doorway. "There's the tower, boy. Now go climb that rope!"

Chapter Ten
Ring the Bell!

While Jake walked towards the bell tower like a prisoner to his doom, Mandy followed Robin to the Great Hall. They ran down halls, ducked around corners, and hid in doorways.

"You seem to know this castle well," she whispered as she tiptoed after him.

Robin smiled. "I do. Before I had to hide in Sherwood Forest, I was a lord. Sir Robin of Lockslee. I was the good king's guest many times."

"Do you still visit?" Mandy asked.

Robin peered around the arch into the hall.

"There is only one reason for me to ever come back here and—" He caught his breath. "I'm looking at her."

Mandy peeked around the corner to see who Robin was staring at.

It was the beautiful lady in the green velvet dress. She was talking to Curtis, who had joined the real court musicians.

"Maid Marian," Mandy murmured. "Of course!"

Robin pulled back and pressed his body flat against the wall. "How did you know that?"

Mandy shrugged. "I saw the movie."

Robin looked confused. "Movie?"

Before Mandy could explain that she'd seen a movie about Robin and his true love, Maid Marian, a trumpet sounded from within the hall.

"All rise for Prince John," a voice called.

"The coronation has begun," Robin muttered. "Where's the bell? That's the signal for my men. We need to hear the bell!"

"I'm sure Jake will ring it any second now," Mandy said. She didn't know whether to run and

try to help her brother or stay and try to find the
owner of the lute.

Meanwhile Jake stood at the bottom of the
bell tower, staring at the rope that stretched into
the darkness of the tower. It was twice as far to
the top as it was in gym class. He was getting
dizzy just thinking about it.

He had heard the fighting in the dungeon.
He had seen a band of Robin Hood's men hustle
Fat Tom into the guardhouse. Fat Tom was tied
up with so many ropes that he looked like a ball
of yarn. Jake had even heard the trumpets that
signaled the start of the coronation. But he still
couldn't find the courage to climb the rope.

Jake was about to give up and run away when
he heard a young boy call to his mother in the
castle's courtyard.

"Mother, they're crowning Prince John!" the
boy said. "How can we stop it?"

"There's nothing we can do, child." The
mother's voice was near tears. "We'll have to work
harder, and there will be less food on our table."

"But it's not fair!" the boy cried. "Can't

someone stop it?"

Without thinking, Jake shouted, "Yes! Yes! Someone can!"

With that, he leaped at the rope and began to pull himself, hand over hand, up towards the bell. "I can do it," he told himself as he climbed higher and higher. "I can do it!"

His shoulders began to burn with pain. Sweat poured down his face and into his eyes. Jake didn't stop to try and wipe it off. Most important, he never looked down. He kept his eyes glued to the bell at the top of the rope. It came nearer and nearer with every pull of his hands. And with every pull he felt stronger and stronger.

When he reached the top, Jake jumped onto the platform next to the bell. He wanted to shout, "I did it!" to the whole wide world. But he had to ring the bell first.

The great brass bell hung from a heavy wooden frame. A wooden hammer sat on the floor beside it. He picked up the hammer and swung it as hard as he could at the bell. The sound it made was so loud that he fell back a step.

Then Jake struck the bell over and over until he thought he'd go deaf.

Down in the Great Hall, the coronation was well under way. The room was full of lords and ladies, all watching silently as Prince John stood before a man in long white robes and a tall white hat. The man held a gold crown covered with jewels above Prince John's head as he said, "The people have chosen John to be their new king, lord of these lands, and—"

The clang of the bell drowned out the rest of the man's words.

"What is that racket?" Prince John demanded as the crowd looked around in confusion.

"That, sir, is a message from the people," Robin called. He leaped into the hall and aimed his bow and arrow directly at Prince John. "You see, King Richard is still our king. And this castle is *still* his home. And that crown belongs to our king, not this imposter."

"Guards!" Prince John cried. "Help me!"

But nobody moved.

Prince John was shocked to see that his own

guards were gone. In their place stood Robin's men with bows and swords raised. Behind them crowded the women and children from Sherwood Forest.

Robin hopped onto a nearby table that had been set for the feast. He lifted a mug and said, "Here's to Good King Richard. Long live the king!"

"Long live King Richard!" the people cheered. The lords and ladies joined in the cheering. Prince John had the crushed look of a beaten man.

As Robin's men ushered Prince John out of the Great Hall, Robin raised his mug again. "And here's to my lady Marian. Still the fairest maiden of them all!"

The beautiful lady in green crossed the floor in one graceful motion. Robin held out his hand and helped her step lightly onto the table beside him.

"Welcome back, Sir Robin," Maid Marian said. "You've been away far too long."

Mandy could swear she saw Robin Hood blush. He bowed at the waist and cried, "This is a new dawn and a new day for our country. It calls for a celebration!"

Maid Marian clapped her hands together.

"Yes, let us have music and dance!"

Curtis and the musicians were just about to start playing when Jake rushed into the room. "I did it, Mandy!" he cried. "I climbed the rope!"

"Yes, I know!" Mandy gave her brother a big hug. "And you helped save the kingdom."

Jake pumped his fist in the air. "All *right*!"

"Maid Marian," Robin said, bowing once again at the waist. "To start this joyous occasion, would you favor us with a tune on your lute?"

Mandy and Jake spun to face each other. "Lute!" they gasped.

"I would love to play for all of you," Marian said. "But my lute is missing. I can't find it anywhere."

Jake and Mandy were grinning from ear to ear as they walked up to Robin and Maid Marian.

"I believe we've found your missing lute," Mandy said, holding it up for Maid Marian to see.

Maid Marian clapped her hands to her mouth. "How wonderful!" she said. "I was afraid I'd never see it again."

As Marian reached for the lute, Jake turned

to the man in green and said, "Thanks, Sir Robin, for this totally great adventure. It's been real!"

Then Maid Marian's fingers touched the lute and Robin Hood, his Merry Men, and the Great Hall disappeared in a flash of light.

Chapter Eleven

The Final Test

In less than a heartbeat, Jake and Mandy were back at the Strange Museum. The rope still hung from the ceiling. The tapestries were still on the wall, but the lute was gone.

"Darn!" Mandy said as the lights stopped flashing. "I would have liked to hear Maid Marian play the lute."

Jake blinked at his sister. "Then we really did meet Robin Hood."

Mandy grinned. "Yes, we really did go back in time 800 years and meet Robin Hood."

"I thought I might have fallen from the rope and hit my head on something," Jake said. He was still feeling a little dazed from the time travel.

"We were in Sherwood Forest," Mandy said, "and we stopped Prince John from becoming king."

"Whoa!" Jake shook his head. "That was amazing!"

"And very scary," Mandy added. "I thought we were going to spend the rest of our days in some awful prison."

"What if we had gotten stuck back in time?" Jake wondered. "It wouldn't be so bad. The Merry Men were pretty cool guys."

"We'd have to hunt our food with bows and arrows," Mandy said, "and live in Sherwood Forest and swing from ropes."

Just the mention of swinging from a rope brought Jake back to the present. "You had to say that, didn't you?" he groaned. "I'd almost forgotten about the big test in P.E. tomorrow. Now I'm really worried."

Mandy stared at her brother in amazement. "I can't believe you are really worried. You just traveled back 800 years in time. You were chased by guys with swords. You were caught in a trap and hung upside down by your ankles in a forest. You helped rescue Robin Hood from prison. And you are afraid of a little rope climb?"

Jake smiled at his sister. Sometimes she was a real pain, but sometimes she was pretty smart. This was one of the smart times.

"Now let's go upstairs," she said, giving him a punch on the shoulder. "Mom and Dad should be waiting dinner for us."

Jake bowed at the waist. "After you, Maid Mandy."

"Thank you, kind sir, but you go first." Mandy stepped back to let him pass in front of her. "And this time, don't touch anything!"

The next day, when it was Jake's turn to do the rope climb, he was smiling. Normally he would be sweating at the thought of what he was about to do. But not today. Jake knew he was going to make it to the top. Two boys before him had tried and fallen, but that didn't shake his confidence. He could do it. He knew it. He was so sure that

he invited Mandy to come watch.

She stood in the gym doors, her camera in her hand. She waved and gave Jake a thumbs-up.

Their adventure with Robin Hood had sealed their friendship. Together they had faced some pretty scary situations. They had both found a strength inside themselves that they never knew they had.

Jake had finally faced his fear of heights. And he was able to help Robin Hood and his friends. Mandy, who normally wilted whenever she was asked to do anything as humiliating as sing or dance in front of people, had performed and loved it. And on top of it all, she had used her wits to get the castle keys from Fat Tom, the giant.

Now Mandy stood beaming with pride as she watched her brother leap onto the rope. Slowly but surely he climbed up toward the ceiling. Just before he got to the top, Jake paused. Several of the boys in the class gasped, thinking that Jake was about to fall.

But Jake didn't. Instead, he whipped off the strange cap that he had borrowed from the museum that morning. Then he waved it at the camera.

Mandy snapped the picture and grinned.

Jake put Robin Hood's green felt cap with the feather back on his head and slapped the ceiling.

He got a perfect score.

About the Authors

JAHNNA N. MALCOLM stands for Jahnna "and" Malcolm. Jahnna Beecham and Malcolm Hillgartner are married and have published over ninety books for kids and teens. They've written about ballerinas, horses, ghosts, singing cowboys, and green slime. Their most recent book series is called The Jewel Kingdom, and it is about adventurous princesses. They even made a movie of the first book in the series, *The Ruby Princess Runs Away*.

Before Jahnna and Malcolm wrote books, they were actors. They met on the stage and were married on the stage, and now they live in Oregon. They used to think of their ideas for their books by themselves. Now they get help from their son, Dash, and daughter, Skye.

About the Illustrator

SALLY WERN COMPORT'S illustrations have been seen nationally for over fifteen years. A 1976 graduate of Columbus College of Art & Design, she began her career as an art director at several agencies before beginning full-time illustration in 1983. Her work has received numerous honors including The Society of Illustrators, Communication Arts, *Print* magazine, *How* magazine, and many Addy awards.

Sally's artwork has been included in several permanent collections, including Women Illustrators from the permanent collection of The Society of Illustrators. Her first children's book, *Brave Margaret*, was released in February 1999. Sally lives with her husband and two children in Annapolis, Maryland.

While the events, locations, and characters described in this book may be based on actual historical events and real people, this story is fictional.